To 媽媽, for teaching me to think outside the book.
To Ingin, for encouraging me to dream inside the book.
— K.Y.

To Jan, my dearest brother and animal lover.
— n.v.

Karen Yin

has never met a blue whale but also worries about fitting in. The founder of Conscious Style Guide, Karen grew up in a public library and spends her days dreaming up better worlds. She lives with her partner and their cat friends on a mountain not too far from Los Angeles, California, USA. *Whole Whale* is her debut picture book.

www.KarenYin.com

Nelleke Verhoeff

started her career performing shows for children, but then discovered her passion for art. She has since illustrated several books and was a finalist in the Silent Book Contest at the 2018 Bologna Children's Book Fair. She loves drawing animals and giving them personality, so this book was a real treat to illustrate! Nelleke lives in Rotterdam, the Netherlands. She has also illustrated *The Bread Pet* for Barefoot Books.

www.RedCheeksFactory.com

WHOLE WHALE

WORDS BY Karen Yin

ART BY Nelleke Verhoeff

Barefoot Books

Step inside a story

An empty page? It's time to play!

The animals are on their way.

One hundred might fit in this tale,
But can we fit a WHOLE BLUE WHALE?

A mink, a moose,
a mouse caboose.
A monkey and a mother goose.

A croc, a hawk, a shark, a snail,

But can we fit a WHOLE BLUE WHALE?

A hippo hoof, a tapir trunk,

A sloth,
       a moth,
            a skink,
                 a skunk.

Here comes a camel and a quail,
But can we fit a WHOLE BLUE WHALE?

So, if they all can get along,

One hundred might fit in this throng.

There's room for more — a beak, a scale —
But can we fit a WHOLE BLUE WHALE?

A pod, a pack, a pride, a prowl —
Just listen to them howl and growl!

Let's make some room! Don't block the trail.

But can we fit a WHOLE BLUE WHALE?

Please, not another ram or rook!
It's way too crowded in this book.

The answer that we must unveil:
How can we fit the POOR BLUE WHALE?

When everybody makes some space,
One more can always find a place.

The **WHOLE WHALE** fits!
They had a plan.
Now count **ONE HUNDRED** if you can.

Can you find all 100 animals?

1 ant

2 bear

3 bee

4 bluebird

5 blue whale

6 butterfly

7 camel

8 cat

9 caterpillar

10 chicken

11 clownfish

12 crab

13 crane

14 crocodile

15 dachshund

16 deer

17, 18 & 19 a *pod* of dolphins

20 donkey

21 dragonfly

22 duck

23 elephant

24 flamingo

25 fox

26 frog

27 giraffe

28 goat

29 goldfish

30 goose

31 grebe

32 hare

33 hawk

34 hedgehog

35 heron

36 hippopotamus

37 & 38 a *prowl* of jaguars

39 jellyfish

40 & 41 kangaroo and joey

42 koala

43 ladybird/ ladybug

44, 45, 46 & 47 a *pride* of lions

48 llama

49 mandrill

50 marabou

51 meerkat

52 mink

53 mole

54 monkey

55 moose

56 moth

57 mouse

58 octopus

59 okapi

60 & 61 orangutan and baby

62 ostrich

63 owl

64 panda

65 parrot

66 peacock

67 pelican

68 penguin

69 pig

70 polar bear

71 poodle

72 quail

73 rabbit

74 ram

75 rhinoceros

76 rook

77 rooster

78 seagull

79 seahorse

80 seal

81 shark

82 sheep

83 skink

84 skunk

85 sloth

86 snail

87 snake

88 spider

89 squirrel

90 starfish

91 stork

92 swan

93 tapir

94 tiger

95 toucan

96 turtle

97, 98 & 99 a *pack* of wolves

100 zebra

Barefoot Books
Bradford Mill, 23 Bradford Street, West Concord, MA 01742
29/30 Fitzroy Square, London, W1T 6LQ

Text copyright © 2021 by Karen Yin
Illustrations copyright © 2021 by Nelleke Verhoeff
The moral rights of Karen Yin and Nelleke Verhoeff have been asserted

First published in United States of America by Barefoot Books, Inc
and in Great Britain by Barefoot Books, Ltd in 2021. All rights reserved

Graphic design by Sarah Soldano, Barefoot Books
Edited and art directed by Kate DePalma, Barefoot Books
Reproduction by Bright Arts, Hong Kong. Printed in China on 100% acid-free paper
This book was typeset in Claire, Jealous Kitty and Might Could Pen
The illustrations were prepared digitally with handmade textures

Hardback ISBN 978-1-64686-163-7 | E-book ISBN 978-1-64686-250-4

British Cataloguing-in-Publication Data: a catalogue record
for this book is available from the British Library

Library of Congress Cataloging-in-Publication Data
is available under LCCN 2020949652

135798642

Barefoot Books
step inside a story

At Barefoot Books, we celebrate art and story that opens the hearts and minds of children from all walks of life, focusing on themes that encourage independence of spirit, enthusiasm for learning and respect for the world's diversity. The welfare of our children is dependent on the welfare of the planet, so we source paper from sustainably managed forests and constantly strive to reduce our environmental impact. Playful, beautiful and created to last a lifetime, our products combine the best of the present with the best of the past to educate our children as the caretakers of tomorrow.

www.barefootbooks.com

Author's Note

We all know what it's like to be left out. It feels pretty awful. And unfair. When the largest animal couldn't fit, what did the others do? Instead of telling the whale she was too big, they all worked together to make the book bigger! We can do that too. We can change the rules and create a more welcoming world — together.

— Karen Yin

Illustrator's Note

The animals in this story wanted to all fit in this book because they wanted to play together. So I began playing with them too! I enjoyed drawing so many different silly animals interacting with each other. I had fun with the sizes of the animals to add more variety — and more playfulness! — to the artwork. Their ability to cooperate and make room for the whale is a beautiful reminder that there's always space for everyone to play together.

— Nelleke Verhoeff